Flash Fiction II

Also by this author:

Flash Fiction

Flash Fiction II

Craige Reeves

VANTAGE PRESS
New York

This is a work of fiction. Any similarity between the names and characters in this book and any real persons, living or dead, is purely coincidental.

Cover design by Polly McQuillen

FIRST EDITION

Published by Vantage Press, Inc.
419 Park Ave. South, New York, NY 10016

Manufactured in the United States of America
ISBN: 978-0-533-15431-9

Library of Congress Catalog Card No.: 2005938975

0 9 8 7 6 5 4 3 2 1

Flash Fiction II

Ceremony

The ground opened at my feet, and maybe another fifty feet across from that. It gripped my guts. I wanted to heave. I'd been in earthquakes—this was global parting. I teetered on the edge of that canyon; hearing; and not being able to grasp the thunderous roar of the Earth ripping open; and jumped.

I jumped in that black tortured ground and fell. I fell for twenty-five or thirty seconds. My prayer? Let my end be fast.

I broke the surface of a deep dark water, knowing it was deep and dark. My eyes were squeezed shut. Thankee Jesus. The second thought: Where am I? The center of the Earth. Jesus.

There were residual vibrations; roars. Mother Earth shook off her ecstasies, and settled again. I dared look. My situation was grim. I must have fallen hundreds of feet. I couldn't see the top of this cavern.

I had landed between two islands, and a muddy, sandy bottom of this pit. Fifty feet to my right, and I wouldn't be scratching this message on this tunnel wall.

I stood and shook, after I swam to the nearest landside. Why? Why did I do it? Because Bob was sterile? Couldn't give me kids? I love Bob. Maybe he'll follow the arrows I've carved. Him or someone.

As far as I'm able to tell, I haven't had anything to eat or drink in two or three weeks. I'm going to use a piece of razor sharp shale on my wrists. It's hopeless. I've no comb; no toothbrush.

1

Ceremony II

I'd found out that Barbara, down in those tunnels 250 feet underground, had no time to carry out her plans with sharp shale. Another quake had torn open the ground at her feet, and this time there was no underground lake to receive her.

There was the rescue team. And there was me, sterile Bob, and wasn't I glad the other members of the team couldn't see me turn beet red. I look at the children from her first three husbands, and I think: did she despair of me?

There were dozens of tunnels in this new area, and the rescuers and I would examine them. I was considered part of the team. We had, unlike poor Barbara, lowered ourselves the two depths. What we found in Chamber 7, twisted my guts and loosened my emotions, to this day still.

Diamonds. There were diamonds as big as Ping Pong Balls. Jesus. My Barbara. My poor Barbara. If she could have stayed alive a while longer, she would have been one of the richest women on Earth.

A Diamond Mine. The earthquake and subsequent earthquake had broken into a vein of diamonds. Geologists say it won't run dry for a thousand years.

As you know the year is 2007. Unless you didn't read the papers or didn't see the news for many years. The Barbara Krenshaw Diamond Vein, is the largest in the world. My Barbara. My poor Barbara.

Star Struck

It was Tuesday. He was supposed to be at the hospital Tuesday. 10:00 A.M. Be at Dr. Wendall's office at 10 o'clock Tuesday morning. He was told the incredible pressure in his lung was (as the x-ray showed) a key. A friggin key! Yes, he slept with his mouth open. Yes, he had a loose parrot that was mad at him. A lot of what happened to Ray Platt that day was my fault. I blabbed about the key. You might say this was something like—someone letting the cat out of the bag!

I'm in Hardwick Penitentiary, and I'll never be released. I'd told Joe Monroe, Ray Platt's mortal enemy, that Ray had swallowed the safety deposit box key, thanks to Kenshaw the Cranky Parrot, in his sleep. He durn near choked on it. The safety deposit box contained 1,000 shares of blue chip stock from a Forbes 500 company worth tens of millions of dollars.

Seems Ray Platt never made it to Dr. Wendall's office. Seems Ray Platt was found in a filthy alley, with his lungs cut open and a bloody linoleum cutter nearby. No key. No safety deposit box key. Imagine That.

Seems the police knocked on my door and said, "Mr. John Platt? Ray Platt's brother? We'd like to ask you some questions."

The Bats

Furry flying rats with teeth as sharp as needles; small like push-pins. Suck and chew a grape down in seconds. We had a laboratory full of them. 1,000 of them. Genetically engineered. Bloodthirsty buggers. Drain ya like sap out of a tree if ya let 'em. Dr. Morris said, "If you keep them in their cages, and in the sealed center, they're harmless." But, I'm Mark Burgess, not Dr. Morris; and it's my job to feed these flying furry rats, with teeth as sharp as needles after a chunk of bloody beef.

Don't look at that. Don't look in your 'mind's eye' what a hungry vampire bat with blood beef looks like. And a hundred of them got loose the morning I was alone in the lab and soon tired. . . .

Well, they fed. They fed on my face and arms before anyone came in and gassed them to sleep. But now, and all the while, I can't say Dr. Morris doesn't have a sense of humor; the stakes went up. Every morning, before any other staff arrive, Henry Morris, Ph.D. draws three tubes of blood from me and makes me take a sleeping pill. I don't say anything. I see how the bats look at the tubes of blood with their tiny red eyes. . . . If I slip and doze off, I'll never awaken and it will have been a quick death. . . . I should maybe feel a little flattered to be thought of as part of an experiment. I keep seeing red-eyed vampire bats attacking bloody beef in my 'mind's eye'.

4

Coffee Break

"Hit me." Bob Reynolds put his stained coffee cup in front of Marge and showed his big gapped stained teeth.

"Whatcha' all doin' afta' work, Baby-Doll?"

"Not climbing in bed with you, Reynolds."

"Well, hey . . ."

Marge despaired. Tuesday night and stuck like a truck. Pouring rot-gut coffee in truckers. Damn.

There's Bill. Withdrawn and sensible. Do yourself a favor, Bill, settle down and marry the next Polly-Anna. There's Joe. Joe can get mean. Marry a gay-divorcee from the city, Joe; and do us all a favor and get your throat cut.

Hey girl! Get a grip on yourself, these are your people. Mary tossed the dish cloth she was dabbing the pastry case with over her shoulder. Tuesday became Wednesday, and the heat did not stop. "Hit me, Marge," and the "Top this off, Marge," went on and on, too.

Give 'em what they want and they'll leave you alone. You might think to yourself, with dogs that might work, but these were the bon-a-fydes. Nightshifts. Truckers. Long Haulers. Give an inch—you might just as well give the whole damn mile.

Marty back there? Pretending to do dishes? Picking his teeth. Next to useless.

All of a sudden, Big Bob Burton came sauntering in. Marge's Biker-Man. "What's it gonna be, Cup-Cake?"

"The usual, Sweetheart." She poured fresh coffee.

5

"How's the meat?" Bob indicated the late night crowd.

"Good. Good." She even managed a smile.

Big Bob Burton winked; and this time the smile was genuine.

Grandpa

"Seventy-five cents?" I was pretending to be angry. My daughter is my everything. "Go ask your Grandfather." Bob Samson, my dad, was sitting in my easy chair, puffing a pipe. I'm Mike Samson, and I knew Dad was listening to us even though he was pretending to watch the news.

"Mary Sampson," Dad was pretending an injustice had been committed, "Won't your dad give you a buck?" "Gimmee a buck." "Gimmee a buck." I warned Dad I was mad now with a look. He shrugged. His look said; "Six years old . . ." So my daughter got her ice cream. And four gumballs. This was later, against my better judgment, but don't try to voice over your father.

And then something extraordinary happened. I told Mary I'd leave a light on for her and she told me to leave one on for myself. Only she said, "Leave one on for you." She was six. Now, fifty years later, I still sleep with a light on. Mary laughs at me. Not meanly. No, not meanly. She knows I yell at night. Thrash. I don't sleep some nights, but wait for the light of day.

Oh god help me.

There's a god-awful pounding. The pounding trip-hammers, too. This I've rationalized; could be my heart. The sleeplessness could be insomnia. The need to have a light on? It's childish. It could be paranoia. Or it could be the way Mary *looks* at me when I smell like tootie-fruitie.

Coffee Club

It began as heh, heh. A few laughs. A joke. Kidding around. Buy six cups—get a seventh cup free. But, coffee isn't a dime anymore. When Dad was alive, maybe coffee was a dime; but coffee is $1.50 a cup minimum nowadays. So, before taxes, you get a 'free' cup for $7.50. Don't forget the seven people who came in out of the cold who saw you sitting there in the coffee shop doing a college assignment. The dish beside the register? Meant for pennies? The one you toss nickels, dimes, quarters in? Because they cause too much jingle in your pockets? The one you fill to overflowing with pocket change?

And when the eye darts to the strategically placed clock to make sure you have *time* for an assignment, do we see a blur of a hand remove 'our' dish to be replaced by a more 'light' dish?

And if you noticed, would you, could you say anything about it anyway? And, did that 'happen' to thirty customers before you? Fifty? Before or after you?

The good news is, you get a free cup of coffee every seventh. The bad news is, don't go in the coffee shop until you've gone to the bank.

Goatee

"Buzz off, Red!" I was talking to what I thought of as a red-neck/racist. I'm a white Anglo-Saxon Protestant, if you prefer. Deeply quietly to yourself; you understand Padré.

'Red' had maybe been suggesting, in just a little too loud a voice, how, (as he put it) "What'd ya' do? Fall on that beard?" I was calm. I could fell bozo with a chop. "It's a goatee."

"Oh, hey," he was talking up. Looking for all the world for some back-up from some of the other red-necks shooting pool. And grab-assing at some of the waitresses; darting between their drunken groping. "We got a educated Beardman!" "I'll tell ya' what, Red." I was going to piss off this hillbilly and I was going to do it on purpose because,

1. It would work to my advantage.
2. I like to cut down big timber.
3. I could.

"You call my facial hair a goatee," I continued, "and I won't have to invoke the curse of the worst thing to hit man since the dinosaurs."

"Whaddya' mean?" Red had been guzzling. He looked at me stupid. Stupid and mean. "I'm winning, Red." The pulse throbbed in his temples. "I'll break your face!"

"Do you know the most famous goatee wearer since the beginning of time?"

I felt ugly. "Lucifer!"

As I said, "Lucifer," I bent at the knees, grabbed the loser's ankles, pulled forward, and more or less ignored him when he came down hard on his coxae/rectum, stunning him.

"Got it, Red?"

The Collection

John Jakes has a collection. John Jakes has a collection of moustaches and he uses them for his altruistic perversions. He'll smell them. Breathe in their 'heady' cheese smells. Their aromas. To him, the orgasmic rotted stench of air left behind, in all its glorified years of having been inhaled over and exhaled over, is mesmerizing. Intoxicating.

And John Jakes has the collection of flesh that was under the mustaches. The upper lips. The upper lips and the moustaches they're connected to. And John Jakes breathes in the rotted flesh stench. Elixir. Perfume. Rotted fungus. Decayed flesh trauma. Delightful. Inimitable.

John Jakes will wear a mustache, as John Jakes works. This is a simple matter of curling his upper lip up over a mustached lip. The work John Jakes engages upon, on moonlit nights in autumn, is Lip Removal.

John Jakes is big. He doesn't want to hurt anyone. He could put an arm around someone's neck and flex; and render a broken neck to so and so. John Jakes has hands the size of canned hams. On moonlit autumn nights, with a rag with chloroform on it, John Jakes comes up from behind Mr. Mustache Wearer, and presses the rag against the nose and mouth of his latest target; at which point, the X-acto knife begins to whistle.

John Jakes thinks he's thinking in his 'inner voice'; "Someone please help me." But he thinks he hears this voice humorously.

The Hill

Trees grew up one side of 'The Hill', and down the other. The Hill is located in Notchwood Park. Notchwood Park is in a suburb located North of Chicago. The Park covers 68 acres of woods, hills, bushes, trails, ponds, and paths. There are green metal streetlights, spaced evenly, every fifty feet. Since 1960, the main rise in land at the east side of Notchwood Park has been known as The Hill. Shaped like an egg, Notchwood Hill has two grassy sides and two wooded sides.

On the east side of the wooded section, there is a path. Lovers Lane. A path that leads to a trail. The trail ends at the bottom of the hill, in a grassy field.

John has awful secrets. Awful secrets he does at night.

"Sing, Sammy."

"Jack and Jill went up the hill . . ."

Sammy is a twelve-year-old boy John caught carving his and his girlfriend's initials in a tree.

John is riding on Sammy's back—piggy-back style. In the dark. Making Sammy sing, 'Jack and Jill' for the third time up the hill. "I'm going to tell my dad."

"Sing, Sammy."

"Get the hell off that kid, you filthy piece of shit!" There was no mistaking this voice of authority.

Sammy's knees buckled and John stood. Three teenagers were standing in the gloom.

"Who's fir . . ." John started. One baseball bat fractured his left elbow, as another bat shattered his right kneecap. A third bat crushed his skull.

Brother

I look back at my facetious, ridiculous anger; my phony bravado, my tough guy nonsense. I look back on it and I shudder. I awaken coated in sweat. Screaming. Yeah, my anger was facetious. I convinced myself; I had a right to be angry. I told myself I was a prisoner of war. I convinced myself I had beat the Mafia for brutality and/or suffered their indignities and tortures. The K.K.K. The State Department, the Justice Department. Yeah, I beat 'em. I beat 'em alright. I pretend I beat these groups and I shudder and scream myself awake, coated in sweat. But, I don't shudder wholly. No, my arms and legs are gone.

I said the Neo-Nazi Third Reich was brought to its knees by one. Me. I said Germany, Russia, Italy, and China fell; for I would not sell out. What is it I wouldn't sell out about? Integrity? Yeah. Honesty? Ahumph. Truth? Uh huh. I wouldn't buy a car. When I had arms and legs—I wouldn't buy a car. The principle of the thing? Maybe. Break the back of the American Dream? Who knows? Stubborn? Put asunder U.A.W.'s? Oh well. There's never been no *Strike*!

I climbed a metal streetlight post. I did it to test my masculinity. I was unscrewing the bulb, when I touched the metal screw area. The shock blew my arms and legs off. Before prostethics. Before sewing parts back on were fashionable.

I sit on my roller board and collect change. Spring,

Summer, Winter, and Fall. I won't sell out the American Dream.

I won't beg.

Water

H$_2$O Aqua. Rain. 40 Days—40 Nights. 40 Pieces of Silver to testify against Christ. 40 years hath the time between World War Two and now. 1945–1985. I don't know why I'm talking about any of this other than to illustrate, there's been blow after tragic blow for civilization over time. We deserve a lot of respect just to have survived until now.

I suppose in the original Biblical times, when the flood waters had receded, New Joy on Earth—Peace to Man. Now maybe because of War, Pestilence, Famine, and Death, and supposedly any and all other Four Horsemen of The Apocalypse; seemingly like a flood of scourge; any hardship should be thought of as what? Heaven? Yes, heavenly. And we now entitle ourselves instead of hardship, with luxury.

A car. A boat. Toys. An officer? Why then, you may just consider yourself entitled to run a business, a factory, a plant. . . . Own a house? Buy a plane? Go ahead. Drink water. Does one drink a lot of water this late in the Twentieth Century as much as a bit of the old brew? And a lot of it? A real giant toga party. You know. Where the Christians were thrown to the lions for grins and giggles? Life expectancy? Zilch!

But now. Now. Now a green pill. Swallowed down with—wa wa. And don't forget your garden variety yellow liquid-oil-based medication injected—hypodermic style.

Liquid? H$_2$O? Aqua? Water? Coffee? Tea? Pop? Soda Pop? Trapped on a desert island with three men, two boys and a case of beer; the desert island ends up with the strongest guy and the beer—if he can only control his insatiable urge to guzzle down the water/alcohol-based beer.

Xxx multiples of millions of millions of said scenarios going on in rooms, apartments, houses, towns, villages, cities . . . pass me a cigarette. . . .

Baseball

"Two men on; bottom of the seventh." "Two outs." "3 and 0 the count." "Haskins delivers." "Swing and a miss." "Strike one." "Three balls and a strike."

Ralph Mungus and Abe Tonile were up above the stadium in the announcers booth calling the game over television. "Well, Abe," Ralph said into the microphone, "will he take one for a walk, or try to hit it?"

Ralph was talking about the batter; getting four balls and walking to first base, or hitting a base hit, maybe, and advancing the runners.

The camera angle suddenly shifted and showed commotion on the visitors bench. Two guys were throwing up, and a third player was coughing violently.

"What's that all about, Ralph?" Abe liked a natural order to things. People scrunched up their faces and the seats began to shake in the bleachers. A loud rattling could be heard in the stadium, and grumbling from the crowd. Suddenly, a bleached, pale, giant slug-like creature was poking its head out of the tunnel leading to the visitors locker rooms.

"What the he . . . ?" started Ralph Mungus. His question was interrupted by a huge mewling screeching. The type of huge mewling screech one would hear if a P-38 Jet hit Godzilla in the guts. Before there would be panic, rampage, the players took the situation to task.

Grabbing up bats, the players pelted the slug with bat

swings. If it felt anything, it gave no indication. The screeching mewling was probably from 'seeing' the sun for the first time.

Well, it stunk, and it took quite a while to clean up the mess; but ya' can't have a big worm eating up baseball fans.

Finally an umpire yelled, "Play ball!"

Work II

The voice in my head was incessant, insistent. "Work the Dummy!" Now I'm the dummy; and as far as I can tell the 'voice' was trying to be funny. Then the voice began to repeat itself. In a sort of lilting sing-a-song type voice. "Work the dummy." "Work the dummy." It didn't scare me to hear the voice repeat itself—it'd done it a lot of times before. It made me mad. Like you want to yell, "Shadd-up!" in your brain.

I'm a writer, and I need my brain for something a little more sensible than a six-year-old Rocco, deep inside me, shooting off his mouth. I'm Rocco Martinez, and I write short stories. I'll write twenty stories in a row; just cruising ahead, full speed, and then I'll hear voices; and I'll cry for ten minutes. I can't understand why. Go figure.

I live in a ground floor apartment, in a small town and I enjoy the occasional distraction of a car door opening or closing outside; or, as I write, a baseball game turned on low. A lot of light. No voice. No voice.

I've written hundreds of short stories. I'll never be Alfred Hitchcock, but I love little stories. I'm pretty smart, and I'm fairly insightful.

I read a book by a favorite author, who informs writers he has a muse in his 'basement.' This muse tells him when, where, why, and how to write. I like this. I like this a lot.

The problem is, 'Little Rocco', I've just thought of, is

calling my brain a 'dummy'! My 'Little Rocco'; my 'voice';
my brain is calling my brain a 'dummy'; at least that's what I
think I'm thinking. . . .

The Sweats

"I'm doing something here; jervous and nerky." My alter-ego protagonist, Gary, was berating me again, if lovingly! "I'm cool," "I'm cool," I assured him backing away, my hands held up protectively in front of me facetiously. Gary was working on his Hog. Dressed Harley. Dressed to kill. This was a bike of bikes.

"You missed a spot." I couldn't help it. One minute the sun was reflected in my eyes, and the next minute this ratchet is flying through the air, about to connect with my right eye. Gary yelled without turning his head. "Get out." "Get the hell out of here!" Gary gets real, real mad.

Gary's a big Teddy Bear, but, that ratchet knocked loose some blood clots, and maybe an embolism or two; or, maybe just a couple of good old-fashioned burst capillaries. That, for me, is when Gary died. That's when Gary signed his own death warrant. Nothing before or after the 'Ratchet Affair' counts.

I have six bloodthirsty pit-bulls and, for exercise, I hang up, let's say six chuck roasts, and let the 'babies' dangle as the blood pours down their throats!

Now enter into the picture, Gary. Ratchet-hurling Gary. My plan included putting Gary in the head-high wooden pen with the 'babies.'

The only thing is, I led the way in. That's when the stroke hit. The door slammed behind me. I screamed once. Crumpled. Gary finished this note.

The Dresser

Tap. Tap. Tap. The cleats on Joey's shoes were clicking loudly on the cement; June 25. Peripherally aware of the sound, Joey whistled tunelessly to himself, in his inner ear, to mask the beating of his heart. He was scared. It was one thing to punk some pimply-faced teenager in the eighth grade, in broad daylight, in front of his classmates; and an altogether different thing to try to hush his foot tapping in an upper-middle class neighborhood at 2 A.M.

It was Carlton. "C'mon, Joey, chug it." The beer was greasy in his stomach and he'd had many too many cigarettes. He was ready to Ralph.

Joey swallowed his heart. "Hold it right there, buddy!" The voice thoroughly chilled Joey. It spoke from the shadows. "Take off your shoes. Take a shit." Joey's response was immediate.

"Take off your shoes, or I'll cut off your feet." The voice was eerily reasonable.

"What the hell are you talking about, man?" Instead of answering the shadow-man was suddenly in front of Joey, grinning through his mustache and goatee; and as far as Joey could tell, naked.

Joey's heart trip-hammered in his heart and as he breathed in sulphur and brimsmoke, and whispered, "Jesus!"

'BBBBZZZZTTTT' "Wrong answer!"

23

Crazy

John was talking to me. I'm Barry Morris. Dr. Barry Morris, John's psychologist.

"I think someone who has 'Amnesia' can't remember the word 'Amnesia.' "

"Why, John? What makes you think that?"

"Maybe it's just an excuse I'm making up for my condition. Denial."

"What's your condition, John?" At this point, John could:

A. Get mad.
B. Clam up.
C. Reveal the truth to himself.

I didn't think John even knew my first name—and that isn't important; as long as John takes his medicine, sees me on a timely basis, and doesn't sweat the small stuff. Besides, I'm genuinely interested in John. I think there's a tiny John McHenry deep inside the John I know; trying to break free and be heard.

"Think about it, Dr. Morris. If I had Amnesia, and couldn't think of the word, Amnesia, I'd say, 'If I had ummmhhh, and I couldn't think of the word, ummmhhh,' I'd be here all day."

He'd broken into a film of sweat. I was patient. He

looked at me askance. He implored me to understand him with his eyes. I kept my face non-committal.

"Maybe I should go . . ." he started.

A tear slid from the corner of his eye and we knew we made progress.

The Sign

A meteor blasted across the sky on August 18, 2008. It was huge. Big as can be. The meteor caused a shadow to cross the planet Earth from horizon to horizon that afternoon and caused the temperature to drop twenty degrees for twenty-eight minutes. What no one knew about were the look-alikes. The look-alikes that 'jumped' on along. First no look-alikes—then millions of look-alikes.

Most of the real 'us' never even knew what was going on. Ectoplasm? Dopplegangers? Ghosts? Yeah. And worse. That and a whole lot worse. Like when you went to the bowling alley to drink, bowl, drink, and you went to have a butt and you got sucked out of yourself and turned to Vapor? Remember that? Or how about that time on the pontoon boat at that party; and all of a sudden you thought you'd urch; and instead you disappeared, along with everybody else? That worse. Right?

And then what? What happened afterwards? When you felt yourself hurtling through time and space, as though on a humongous comet or meteor, and **HUNGRY?** nay; *Starving* for stability. **YEARNING** to do nothing other than to settle in a nice quiet place to be a gentle soul; remember? Or do you still remember being sucked from without of yourself, huh? Vaporized!

And after the fuss, after the muss, the meteor tale? The

heat wraithe that bombarded you through and through de-
pleting sweat glands, tear ducts, tongue moisture?
Ooohhhh, aaaaahhhh, meteor . . .

The Sign II

Then, after Earth, another planet inhabited, colonized. Ah, we won't be sucked up in doppelgangers now! We won't be vaporized or hurtled out of time and space by some comet tail now.

No, we go to Alien Finders Dot Com. Ghost Shrug Off. Net. Don't we learn that when a mysterious comet is in our area, we are safe in our basements, if the upstairs has plenty of aluminum foil?!? Yes, we may *feel* like we're going to Ralph, but are we? Are we going to spew a warm stew? And, after all, how bad are these Aliens? Oh, boo-hoo, we had to move. We got implaced. I've got a friend who says who cares? So what? And who does care??? Who cares if we move from one planet to another every once in a while? Huh? Or get our place taken? But, is my (buddy) an original?

And something else occurs to me. Did you ever hear of Idjun-Pidjud-Lay? 'Pig Latin'? Well, I've got an inordinate desire to hit the streets and yell at the top of my voice, "Chuck-You-Farley!" And things like that. Yes, it's true enough; I'm keeping this written testimonial of *The Comet* and events concerned.

And it's also true enough The Cabinet of Vice Ministry of Peace said, no public execution for me like so many other tens of thousands.

A–Z

"Aye, Bee, Cee." Jane was saying the alphabet in the best way she knew how. Very clearly. Very concisely. Very correctly. Jane said the alphabet, and she said the alphabet, to a V.I.P. Jane knew a 'V.I.P.' was a Viper In Person. Jane was telling the alphabet to an Alien. Martian? Velutian? Jane was six years old.

The A-PoP-O-Crypsye had happened, and Jane was in charge. Jane was in charge because she could spell. Jane could do a lot of things; but she wasn't going to do what she knew in front of what Billy called 'The Brass.' Jane could get the Viper out of the Alien, but it had to go to sleep.

Then she had to dangle a piece of raw meat over its mouth. Six-year-old Jane figured, if that worked for 'tapeworms' it would work for a snake. This was an 'Old Wives Remedy.'

The thing was what difference did it make if the Alien had a snake or not? It still couldn't talk. No vocal cords. Little Jane Austin would say the alphabet to this little green Martian until she was blue in the face—it wouldn't talk. Snake filled or not. And the Rascal would drool up to its eyes all day long—and not say anything.

But she wouldn't say anything either. Not say anything. She thought she was seeing things the first time the Martian swallowed a mouse whole. She really brought it back up, swallowed it again until a snake slithered after it—into the Alien's mouth!

29

Red Alert

Aliens. Aliens. Aliens. All these fricken' aliens are going to be the death of me yet. Some six-year-old brat back in 2012 taught the fricken' alphabet to these stupid goulies, too. And comets hurtling by are now a common event. Oh, oh, oh, what of this can I bear?

A lot of what happened; us human types were exploited. Humans. These aliens pretty much have us over a barrel; we didn't resist. They kinda' have us in a grip of our short-hairs. Nuts. What of this can I take? They colonized IN us. Zap; Bob—you're Moono the Alien. Well I'm going to go down fighting. I'm going to kick some alien ass! We fought the Arabs, Turks, and Saudis and we did okay. Okay.

Hey listen up; if I can't get some attention from the *Silent Majority* out there, what the hell kind of fight am I going to put up?

I've got a few plans. One plan is to turn bat-spiders from the dark side of one of the Moons of Jupiter from troublesome to trouble-shooters. Have them get in a feeding frenzy for the fresh stink of alien meat. A bat-spider will turn a human inside out within moments. They will, I've discovered, devour an alien like a man eats a grape. Squish. This is war baby—and don't you forget it; maggot!

There can be no loose threads. If you can't keep up—you're cannon fodder! We have one big secret these aliens don't seem capable of surmising—the few for the many! If caught low, I drink gas and ignite myself! See how they like that!

III

By God and by golly I'll get out of this booby-hatch; and I'll have it made and then there'll be no one who can do uhhhnhhh about it.

First it began with Tasers. That brought us to our knees. Oh, ahyup! Hurt our knees a pretty bit too. Then came the treatments. In the early days they strapped you down. As time went scaddling along they sedated you and regulated the amounts of voltage coursing through your body. Big guy? A bit more. Ankle bracelets. Make you walk like you got a lightning rod stuck up your arse when you're zapped, unexpected like. Like Lurch. We all know a Lurch.

The 'Collar.' It began as a word to describe bringing down a perp or perv. Now? Nod your head up and down and do it with a shit-eating grin or I just won't let go of the 'trigger.' Man's inhumanity to man. And on and on it goes.

Static electricity? Don't make me laugh. Then again, in the Winter? Surrounded by snow? In its basic breakdown, water?

Snap, crackle, pop. You said you blew a fuse? An' 'lectric belts? Eh heh eh heh eh heh.

31

Webber

Now we did it! Yeah, we did it all now! We had hung wires, razor thin wires over our parking lots. Why? Why to keep birds off our precious tarmac. Don't soil my cart, you nasty bird, you! And we hung wire to enhance the halogen lighting out into the dark night—as reflectors. And I suppose these wires would heat under the glow of the sun and high intensity bulbs of halogen lights; lowering the amount of perhaps some snowfall?

But there's a dissenting voice in the ensuing milieu? Yes, there's a dissenting voice.

Yes, we had done wrong. Wrong. Wrong. Wrong. A taut wire will thwart a bird from landing where there's a taut wire for fear of having a wing shorn off. Even no bird ain't stupid.

But a nighttime bat-spider from the light side of the moon of Jupiter will see wires hung over a parking lot as a what? A Web? Yes, I can see a bat-spider from the light side of the moon of Jupiter as seeing wires hung over a parking lot as a Web.

And a bat-spider hardly has no compunction about gripping a body in its seemingly unbreakable grip of mandibles and carrying it up into *layers* of wires *it* had subsequently Woven—God bless us one and all, Tiny Tim.

Oh, Jesus. I hear those awful hideous screams when I go down to the Mall for a loaf of bread. And I hear begs of mercy being shouted for when I walk the dog down at the ball park. God Have Mercy!

Yeah, seems there ain't hardly any bird doo on the car windshield nowadays. Seems the bat-spiders from the light side of the moon of Jupiter took care of that little problem.

Good Fun

There is some strange business that goes on under the bleachers in a ballfield. Racetrack. Park. Sometimes the guys will get their gal under a tree or bench and smooch. Drink. Pet. Smoke some pot. Well, none of that happy nonsense for me. No sir. Oh, I have a girl and I'm real glad to have her boss.

There's an abandoned warehouse behind the old railway district on the west side of town. They tore a lot of those old warehouses down, but there's plenty still left.

Every year I challenge myself. When crisp fall air is blowing dead leaves up cold streets under dark skies, I go in a warehouse. It's the same warehouse. The same as the nightmare. Halloween. The houses with porch lights and jack-o-lanterns with the candle flames blowing this way and that, left far behind, I enter. It reeks.

It's pitch black. It stunk the first time I came here but now, it's what the kids call 'ripe.' Nighttime finds solace in the darkness here. It's cold though no wind blows. You can see your breath—if you can see.

"Over here a kid." The voice breaks through the warmth you deluded yourself into thinking you had felt. You choke back a scream. In rags that had once been clothes, a beggar stumbles closer. His breath is sour gin and vomit. He reaches out a half gloved hand and seductively whispers, "Do you like it here?" You want to run. You want to retch. He moves the hand downward. You begin to shake. You wish you had a length of pipe to bash at him.

"C'mon kid. I'll give ya' five bucks and make ya' feel good."

Day by Day

Day by day I'm growing stronger. Just last week Barbara wouldn't have been able to drag me within a block of that tenement. The tenement is abandoned. Deserted but for the winos, rats and cockroaches, that aren't particular about what company they keep.

Barbara is my light. My reason for making the effort to continue living. I have a few maladies. Agoraphobia is one of them. Fear of open places.

I was fine until I was maybe twenty-five or so. I'd challenge myself to come to these rotten tenements in the cold of Autumn and collect myself.

Hyperemia is another of my troubles. Hyperemia is a large amount of blood accumulated somewhere in your body. Mine is in the carotid artery, in my neck.

When I was maybe twenty-five, maybe younger, I seem to remember having done *nasty* things. Then the light of day being shunned by me. Nighttime seemingly more welcome by the night.

Night sounds. Cats growling in heat. Hideous anger a male should attempt a mounting!

Cold air. Cold air to chill the blood in your veins. The smell of soil, bats and rats.

Barbara is my light, but day by day she is evermore more listless. Subdued and pale. Drained and dragging through life, looking!

The Hat

"It's a fishing hat, dip-shit." I was talking in my mock French/Angry voice to my 'Pi son' Gary. "Wow." I'd have to fish a response from him. "Who cares?" He has the aggravating habit (if lovable) of trying to put you down if you didn't have a strong offense. "Look, Gary, you can put your favorite flies and lures around the rim." "Who cares?"

I share my enthusiasm of the new, the different, the exciting, among other things with Gary, as I think maybe half the time he has a migraine or a severe toothache or some-such thing. Ulcer? And maybe he's a big softy. The gruffness masks pain? Gary's as proud as they get, too. Don't try to play it too sweet with Gary.

"Whatcha' gonna do with it Bubba-Bug?" He'd a nick-named me himself. I had to hide a quick smirk I had coming on. I was thinking, Gary was thinking, I'd give him the hat. And besides, Gary could read me like a book—and he'd known I'd been thinking he'd been thinking that.

"I want to have a 'Fish-off.' "

"A what?"

"A fish-off. Like a chili-cook-off, but with fish."

"It's your ass, Bubba-Bug."

He wears the hat with some of his favorite lures when he knows I'm down-in-the-dumps. I hooked my left eye in the fish-off. I ruined Gary's whole day.

The Flight

We were going unconscious. Altitude. "Ladies and gentlemen," the stewardess had intoned at the start of the flight, her pearl white teeth between thin, bright red lips, in stark contrast to her almost pitch-black hair, continued, "if we experience at any time any loss of control of flight 718, an oxygen mask will quickly drop down from the compartments, directly above your heads."

That was forty minutes ago that seemed like 40 hours. I don't know to this day what the hell made me feel like I needed to be a hero at that moment. We'd hit turbulence at what was last announced as 39,000 feet. And the flight began to climb. Climb. Climb. Climb. I remember thinking, as the oxygen mask compartments popped open, it's a fight or flight situation. And I broke into a shit-eating smirk as I shouldered open the forward cabin.

Everyone else had buckled up as per instructions over the public address system.

The pilot, co-pilot, and navigator were slumped over their controls. Only the controls weren't pushed forward. They were in the backward position! First I leaned the pilot, co-pilot, and navigator in the upright position. Secondly, I gently, ever so gently, eased the controls forward. Thirdly, I placed the oxygen masks back over the faces of the crew. After several anxious seconds of not knowing what to expect, the crew came about, and no harm befell us.

Hoo Doo

Now gimmee a little credit here. If somebody offers you a choice of taking ten dollars or twenty dollars, you'll snatch that twenty dollars faster than the naked eye can blink. But suppose the guy offering the twenty dollars (as opposed to the ten dollars) says, "If someone offers you a chance to take twenty dollars or ten dollars—take the twenty dollars!?!" Does that make you a sucker?

No, I'm afraid that makes the person handing out the loot a sucker.

Now lend an ear. Maybe the guy had a good reason to give out money freely. Not to make a sucker out of himself, or to make you greedy. To be a good samaritan? Maybe. To be vain and proud and conceited? Possibly. But let's look at some bigger pictures. Philanthropy? Okay. Gregarious? Sure. But how about having a trade wheeling and dealing, and being master of none?

Then said Joe Blow, a Hoo Doo? Hanger-onere; wanna-be leech? Unwise about money AND giving IT away.

There's a word about having money to make money. Well, if you have a bundle of money you could reasonably expect to have vast bundles of money, if it takes money to make money and you don't give it all away.

So you take your bundle and you pass it about; and you begin to amass a large bundle of money. And just as good as all this money, you begin to make friends. Lots and lots of

39

friends. Organizations. And before long you're one happy camper and you have made many, many people happy.

And you've soon forgotten being a Hoo Doo.

Snail Control

They were under the stadium. That's what the reporters said; they were under the stadium. The stadium by the sea. Sea snails as big as man. And quick-quick. Fast as Centipedes. Growing. Waiting.

"Man on first; two outs." "Three and 'oh'; the count." "Batter swings." "It's a two out; two run; home run!" Under the locker rooms. In the catacombs under the bleachers. The Club Houses.

From the slimy water first crept slimy snails. Eating such exotics as rats, half eaten/half forgotten peanut butter and jelly sandwiches, but first, cockroaches, ants, spiders. Growing. Waiting.

Big now; slinking in the sea. Game done and over. Fog cover? Certainly a part moon to guide these snail/slugs along their slime trails. The players confident in their game suits.

"Play ball." A new day. The snails restless under the stadium. The 'telescopic' eyes on their stalks; quivering. The snails' maws salivating prove man's myth about snails and salt, unaccountable as they eagerly await the salt-sweat dripping off a careless grounds-keeper's torso; being dragged kicking and screaming through passages of dark dread.

Whimpering death below. A collective shout of "Hurrah!" from above as a home-run is scored. And slushing sounds of slime in rolling agitation. Slime-coated boulder/bricks where human sweat had accumulated over the millennium is slurp/sucked off. Bones sucked white. Girls and boys. Men and women.

Someone, sometime, somewhere, will call Snail Patrol. In the meantime, the skulls grin their screams; and the umpires yell, "Batter-Up!"

The Pain

There is a 'pain-scale' in your local doctor's office. On one end of this scale, (the left side) (the beginning) there is a smiley-face; with the mouth turned right-side up, all happy and aglow. But on the right side of the pain scale, there is a smiley face whose lips are pressed down in a frown. There is a numerical chart, as well; one being the least amount of pain—ten being the greatest amount of pain.

Not a patient comes in and is asked, on a scale of 1–10, how they feel; that they don't announce invariably, between 9–10. This from a bonafide doctor. Swear to God. And again, invariably, this doctor is thinking, if your four limbs are cut off, honey, then you're 10 on the pain scale; maybe just if all your digits are missing. Otherwise—buzz off. I wonder the wisdom of not at least coddling this patient; the way he says he feels.

Some ways of disease are terminal with a lot of horrendous pain thrown in for grins and giggles. Maybe withdrawal symptoms. Quitting drugs or booze can feel devastating; wherein all comfort able to be provided, should be provided. Malpractice might be another reason to be aware of chronic pain/symptoms. Wrongful torture? Wherein death in these cases could be a claim for 'Assisted-Suicide?'

As far as I can ascertain, the primary 'Golden Rule' of 'Doctoring' is to do no harm; wherein you can do no good. Now, what are you smiling about?

Survivor

I'm that daffy old bird that was making marks on the trees in the jungle. Man, what a time THAT turned out to be.

'They' said when they found me, I had twenty-five diseases. Twenty-five. Dear me. Dear 'O' Dear 'O' Dear 'O' Dear. They said I was out in that there jungle 37 years. 37 years. Imagine. I tried to imagine it and I couldn't. And it happened to me! Lord 'O' Lord 'O' Lord 'O' Lord.

After awhile, I started to find notches and gouges out of trees. Sometimes they made sense to me and sometimes they didn't make any sense to me. The gouges and notches went down one path—and came up another. My 'O' My 'O' My 'O' My.

Well, I suppose you're wondering what the My 'O' My and Lord 'O' Lord is all about. Like I said, I was in that god-forsaken jungle thirty-seven years. A man can get good and lonely in thirty-seven years. Well, I married a native woman. And we raised three sons and two daughters. And I will NOT say, B y 'O' B y 'O' B y 'O' B y. I just won't. No, I won't do that.

I'm daffy and I'm a quack, but my sons can run 100 miles with spears and knives and a little flask of water and a little pouch of food and fight to kill or be killed asking no/and giving no quarter! Along with 600 million other natives. That was quite a day.

What was I talking about?

Survivor II

I've been back in civilization twenty-two years, and now I'm beginning to remember a little something about my L. B. J. (Life before Jungle). I didn't used to curse, and if I did, I quickly forgave myself by answering up the curse word with the one-word questions—Who, What, Where, When, Why, How. At least mentally.

Well, it seems what with twenty-five odd diseases one of them was Malaria. Well, again, it seems that with Malaria, you have a tendency to be barely cognizant of your surroundings, what you're doing or saying in the deep throes of this malady.

It seems for up to and including four of the twenty-two years back world-wise, I was gibbering in a loud, incoherent voice; Who, What, Where, When, Why, How. With no one having the least little idea why I was doing that. And I wasn't even aware I was doing it. And then, when the quinine water took effect my superstitions of curse words came out. And that took six months of explaining. Because a lot of times words would come out like F***; Who, What, Where, Sh**; Who, What, Where, When, Why . . . Yeah; that there took a little while . . . Quite a while.

The Game

It was getting hard to concentrate. It was getting hard to concentrate, but that's what Nemo wanted. He wanted you confused and full of anxiety. Scared and paranoid. You weren't supposed to know you were on or sliding and falling down on ice.

He took our eyes. As far as I know there were four of us. He took our eyes. Ears. Tongues. Nemo took our eyes, ears, tongues, noses and hands. And by doing that, Nemo made us without remorse, humanity or concern. The four of us wanted simply one overwhelming desire: survival.

We were bundled in huge parkas of the sort issued in drastic circumstances. Care of Uncle Sam. Boots in boots. Thermal socks. Two pair. Catheters in urethras, with colostopy bags for the 'other.' Nemo or his goons saw to the emptying twice a week. Hats. Face mask hats so the Antarctic frost at minus seven degrees split our skulls open with frigid perma-oxygen in them. Yeah, we had pants and shirts—Carhardt. And we put gloves over the stumps where our hands used to be. To what end?

Nemo instructed, "Move around; you won't feel quite so cold." But what little Nemo didn't count on, I had a plan. Watch survival guy trek across Antarctica.

I trundle about trying to trip up one of us. Crush his/her face against this glacier. Kill it, as it has no humanity, remorse, concern left to note as a he or she. I've killed two? If I can find no other, I'll unclothe myself. . . .

Bumper

The knocking was coming from the cell on the left. I could sense the vibrations in the air. We were the experimental. Nemo had us in captivity in Antarctica for three years. We are kept in cells, when we are not forced to trudge through the frozen/frigid wasteland outside. As I said, Nemo took our eyes, ears, noses, tongues, and hands. If these gruntings into this tape-recorder (which I know Nemo placed on this table in my cell by feeling with my forearms) are ever interpreted, I want you to know I must be killed. I'm beyond insane. I can't bear what that bumping, next cell over is telling me. Kill me. Kill me. Kill me. That's what the poor creature wants. To be killed.

But I can't see. Is it Nemo or his goons tormenting me? I try to crush who falls or stumbles outside on the frozen wasteland outside; but, are they dead? Does Nemo put a corpse under my boots to trample?

A time back, I thought I would remove my clothes to expose myself to the elements and die. But how? How could I so much as remove my hat? I must leave open a part of my garments in here, so that maybe when I'm made to go outside—I die. Instantly.

I got the patrol of the cells sort of figured out, so I'll scrape off the bottoms of both my inner and outer pair of boots and hope for the best. Oh dear God; that bastard cut off my feet!!!

Bumper II

"Move around, you won't feel the cold so much," Nemo had instructed. What Nemo didn't know was I had a plan. I sort of knew Nemo had a helicopter to hunt us. (Keep track of us.) "They" hunt Caribou? Polar bears? Yeah, move around. Mad bastards cut off my feet. But I can hobble on snow-shoes. I was too preoccupied. Did they sedate me and do it? Or was I too too preoccupied to pay attention? Too nuts to know they were cutting my feet off, awake? Is that unthinkable?

I had a plan before my feet were removed. Now plan 'B'. Plan 'A' was to kill my fellow travelers. Across the frozen wasteland. Plan 'B' included throwing myself into the path of a water-cooled .30 cal. machine gun slug Nemo now spits down on us from the chopper. I knew he was doing THAT as a chunk of ice thrown up on our leg or arm or somewhere, despite the extra thick clothing, as a warning to stay away, or back from somewhere would leave a festering sore for a couple of weeks.

Herding. Nemo was herding us for a past-time. God knows how many polar bears and wolves he kept at bay. I ask myself if being eaten by starving wolves wouldn't be more merciful than being in Nemo's 'keep'?

To have Nemo shoot 50 slugs at me in mere seconds I was going to have to be a bear. Look from above; like a polar bear attacking one of Nemo's puppets.

Nemo communicated to me later he never knew just

what I was up to. For twenty days I breathed in and out of my mouth. I could now smell the guy—next cell over. When I was sure the chopper was overhead I sliced my throat with a butter knife I had secreted out of the quonset hut, by holding my forearms together. And I struck. I smelled my victim. I kicked up snow. And I knew I was splashing blood everywhere.

Nemo landed the chopper, gave me stitches, and didn't do a damn thing. He has some sort of other plan. Jesus . . .

Bumper III

So okay, Nemo doesn't care if I stomp one of his other 'puppets' to death; unless, he did get upset and that's why the bastard cut off my feet. I still reserve the feeling I'm fulfilling a need for Nemo here.

What I think a lot about is, because I was trying to cut off the bottoms of my boots, Nemo got mad. Stomping the other travelers to death didn't matter.

He doesn't want us (me?) to hurt ourselves. If I'm quite the burnout Nemo is trying to make me believe myself of being, I'm liable to think ships float upside down and inside out, too. I'll tear somebody apart—but don't let anybody hurt themselves.

And now there's more bad news. Wicked news. I see light—even though my eyes are gone. I take great comfort from this.

Wicked news. Oh, yes. Chips and chunks of frozen/frigid ice has been striking me with increasing frequency. Hitting the same places my body, two sometimes three times in a row. It causes me to despair. Trudge. Trudge. Suddenly, thoroughly drenched and weightless, the ice/frozen/frigid 'ground' from under me (us?) is replaced by an open glacier lake! Jesus. A rope thrown over our shoulders and dragged behind a snowmobile? The guy next cell over, "Kill me, kill me . . ." Stumps for feet. Driving us like cattle—but what more of this can I take? What more?

Nemo gave me two cheeseburgers and french fries and a coke. I was crying so hard I couldn't eat them. . . .

Johnny and Squirt

The last me and Squirt heard, they had locked Mrs. Samson in some loony-bin up north. Guess what? The deer? The road kill? Mrs. Samson had killed it with a knife. Our Mrs. Samson was patient. If Mrs. Samson was anything, Mrs. Samson was patient. She waited for the deer. She waited and she cut its jugular vein and she bled it like the water buffalo in Asia. Carefully tracking the drops of blood. Carefully waiting until she could slam her 'ol man with his favorite crowbar. Patiently waiting for the paperboy. Arsenic cookies? A little spiked Kool-Aid for the postman?

She was put in a loony-bin upstate and waited. Waited. Waited. Waited.

It was in the papers. The fire in Westwood Home for the Criminally Insane started when the gas jets of the old-fashioned burner stove were all left in the 'on' position with the pilot lights blown out. The fact that the twelve burners were left on unnoticed and subsequently unquestioned was not lost on me and Paulie. We followed the story carefully. Two days after the fire, a cow had been killed and chunks of meat bitten out.

Paulie and I had grown. We lived in an apartment. Ma and dad lived two blocks away.

"Will she come for us, Johnny?"

Paulie's not stupid. "Yeah, Squirt, she'll come for us. She's nuts. We're safe."

I awoke that night to a butcher knife at my throat. I'd

never heard a sound. It was Mrs. Samson. "I want my road kill." Her breath was sour pickerel. She suddenly collapsed on top of me.

"I hit her. I hit her, Johnny." Paulie was dancing in the moonlight from an open window with a bat with a wet top.

Re-assembled

Red Fred. Red Fred. More like, Dead Fred. When I get my hands on Red Fred, he's dead meat. Of course, he's only a skeleton and already dead, but it boosts my courage to 'see' in my mind's eye me pulling Red Fred's skull off of his spindly umbligata and/or spinal cord. And it helps me to write down what I'm going to do to him, too.

I'd gotten the story from Murray, human reject one. Murray had been told that Red Fred and some of the other skeletons and skel-bots had dunked some fresh skeletons and skel-bots in a flat smelter. Skeletons and skel-bots who stand around from eon to eon.

Red Fred had told Murray this little bit of business, and I immediately knew why. Murray ain't the smartest human in the steel mill, and, thereby, given to wild imagination. Figuring maybe what it felt like to feel hot slag running up and down your arms and legs, might spur slow Murray to talking to co-workers; that maybe the Skeletons are on the march. That maybe you're next? A lot of people know that beyond a shadow of a doubt a skeleton won't touch a human. Not since the human skel-bot wars. Explain THAT to somebody scared out of his wits. We let Murray go. We gave him a gold cigar. Recommendations. A retirement account. Things returned to normal.

Problem is, some of these skeletons running round were wearing a little skin in the chest area. Gristle, blood, and skin in the chest region. She-Bots. Jesus Fred! She-Bots?

The Prize

Yeah, yeah, yeah: I was collecting mouhlah—and I was digging THAT action, bigtime. But I was collecting mouhlah in a way the police might say was 'illegally.' A priest might call immorally. Strong arm. Put the muscle on a 'dupe.' Put the 'squeeze' on a punk. String out some punks—for their own good, of course.

I won the lottery 10x10 times—and I got a rush every time. Some people call me a goon. That's true. Some people say my face would stop the five o'clock express. That's true. They say these things in a low voice behind my back. Big men scuttle across the street when they see me coming.

I'm dictating this in traction. The prognosis—death. My neck is crushed. Diagnosis? Life support. Tube feeding. Tubes inserted in lungs. I admit, I'm a moose. I'm as big as hell and I want this death penalty. Do you know the inglorious shame of a big hog like me; crapping in a bedpan? Oh, Jesus. Let me finish my story. A friend said, "C'mon over, I got a surprise for you." Well, my buddy lives on a hillside—but I'll get back to that.

"A book. You wrote a book about me?" I didn't know whether to shit or go blind. I went for the defensive. "What the hell did you go and do that for?"

"I thought it would make you happy," Jonesy squeaked, looking a little pale.

"It pissed me off. I'm going to take a leak and then me and you are going to burn this piece of shit."

When I came out of the bathroom, I should have seen the gleam in his eyes—that he was flushed.

The car was under a streetlight and God help me, I didn't notice the minute movement of the tires. I saw the glimmer of a quarter sticking partway under the car, though. . . .

Buggy

No doubt. There was an infestation of the No-See-Ums. That's all. No-See-Ums. The corpse had not bloated. It didn't stink. There was no discoloration. Just all those countless No-See-Ums in the tens of thousands. Flittering forth and back. Back and forth.

They were as an undulating black carpet on her pale, unarguing skin; and I stared. I stared and I grew erect and I'm horrified and I'm ashamed of myself—but I ate her alive with my stare. I couldn't remove my glare. She was naked. She lay face-down and she was crawling with the No-See-Ums. It got worse. My condition grew worse.

After being in her house with her the 500th time/ 700th? Dead still, but for the moon shadows at night; alive at day; silent; but crawling with life. No smell, no discoloration, no bloating, I wanted to *be* her.

Young. Younger than life. Inside out young. No faire—no foule. There there. All and nothing at once. Full and empty. After being with her the thousandth time, I grew stronger. We grew stronger. We danced. We dined at her twelve guest dining room table. I carried her upstairs and bathed her. I did unspeakable acts to and for her. With her. And mostly she agreed to them; and from time to time she disagreed to these acts, at which time I would violate her. Sometimes she would agree and at other times, disagree.

The No-See-Ums stay with her. They have no part of me. They're for her. They're hers. If something dead can possess. Take care of your No-See-Ums. Your No-See-Ums will take care of you. It's what she has.

I don't cramp her style and she doesn't step on my toes. The worse things get, we stare each other down. We talk and laugh and cry after a fight. I feel strange fighting with her. Maybe it's a little 'Buggy.' I'm *mainly* okay.

Toast

I can feel it coming. There's going to be trouble. I can feel it coming. The 'voices' say, "Go back in. Go back in the Army." I'm a paraplegic, but I could teach a survival course or any number of other courses. Then another 'voice' says, "Forget it, Murcer, you're chewed up and spit out; and nothing but your lonely shadow wants you for company."

So, I'm sitting in this bar and a guy says; "Hey, ya only got one leg!" Usually I tell them I'm letting someone else use the other one. It was kind of cool though. This rummy thought it was unique. I could tell from his intonation. It got blown off. It was all I could think to say, and it was true.

"No shit! Army?"

"Yeah."

He had a deep voice, like a trucker or a warehouse foreman.

"Look, Pal." He was looking me eye to eye, man to man, and I was suddenly creeped. "We are going to be with each other for awhile. We are going to get to know each other," he decided. He changed directions. "Bartender. Drinks. Me and Scotty here."

"No, count me out . . ." I started.

"Bullshit," he countered easily. "Nothing's too good for the Army."

"Look, mister . . ."

"George."

"Okay, George, I'm not going to have a drink with you."

"Yeah, Scotty, You'll drink. You'll drink 'till ya can't stand up, fall down, get up, or have somebody help ya get up. You'll roll over and beg just like the rest of us. Whimper and wag the dog. Right, Smitty?"

This time he was addressing the bartender, but his voice had risen and the other customers were looking our way and suddenly he raised his glass; looked me in the eye and said, "TOAST!"

Downside

We've all heard it all before. There's a downside to every-thing. Hello. Like there's a bright side to everything. Duhh. Like the lights are half on, *and* someone is home. Errrhhh.

I got this bad issue working me. Good scenario, bad sce-nario. I feel like a bottom feeder in this situation. I was in Viet Nam and there was a saying about if you did someone wrong—backstabbing. There was a song about it too. Well, I feel good, most of the time, but sometimes I'll back-attack somebody senselessly. Why? I'll blame back-attacking on a good number of things. Brain damage. Schizophrenia. Agent Orange poisoning. Revenge. How do I live with my-self? By saying to myself I had a serious drinking problem. Or I was heavily medicated. Sorry, I blew your son away, it's 'cause I take medicine. My back was up against the wall. These excuses won't bring anyone back.

We're not here to talk about the good and bad that went on with me. Not specifically. What I want to tell you are ways to guard against back-attacks. Backstabbing. A good sports agent would have you know; a good offense is a good defense.

A law enforcement officer might advise you, Silence is Golden. A soldier might be warned to gird his loins. (Bibli-cal) May I submit, walk tall, but carry a big stick?

Yeah, Bro, there's a 'downside' to business as usual. I tried to keep a stiff upper lip when I bit the throats out of those sixteen people I 'downsided'; I tried to keep a stiff upper lip, but I can't stop laughing. . . . I can't stop laughing about it. . . .

Pound Puppy

My guess is I had 'it' rough. Life. Yes, life. I had life rough.
Very bad.

When I wasn't being 'worked' on, my arms were put
behind my back of the back of a length of branch, and
brought forward at the elbows; then my wrists were lashed
to a branch placed behind my thighs. I was hit; beaten;
punched in this position; but for my head. My head was un-
damaged by blows from fists. That was left for 'Buddy'.
'Buddy' is a doctor. A mad doctor. When he's in a fair mood
'Buddy' will tell you in a voice over-riding your piercing
shrieking, he's mad. I was lucky. I was made to have a body
wrapped around pain. I was given to pray for more. Buddy
straps you to your metal table with its attendant
blood-trough running around it to 'work'.

As work was done, it was very important to make no
noise. No sound. They'd taken my tongue, eyes, ears, and
nose. I'm guessing they wanted to remove my mind intact,
outward of my skull. If I made noise, I was burned and
shocked until I was silent. Work was kept up on me months
at a time. I sensed pieces of my skull being *taken.*

No reason to pray for mercy; if you were 'perceived' as
in devotion in some introspective fashion, you were shot.
Shocked? You were shot in a part of your wreckage of a
body that was not life threatening. Being shot, other, than
the 'blunt-trauma,' was its use afterwards. A finger poked
around inside a bullet wound might put a damper on any

suggestion about mercifulness for maybe up to and including one full minute. Yeah, quell that prayer notion.

So I got away and alerted the press. I did, did I not? The uglies with whom I suffered torture and torment galore made and broke camp three or four times a month. This for survival? They run miles. Miles. Set camp. Break camp. Run miles; set camp. There were ten thousand of these goulies. On one breaking of camp—I broke. I broke away. I knew nothing of death—how close, what manner—and I cared not.

I tore myself almost apart and was found by Christian mercenaries. Tapping my skin, me tapping back, we communicated this story.

Pipes

I took to thinking, every time someone starts a car, how much carbon monoxide is emitted. Now look, I'm no Ralph Nader. I'm not an agent for Greenpeace. I'm not an environmentalist. I'm not even a pet owner. I'm a nonsmoker who strongly *guesses* when a car, boat, plane, motorcycle, are started—and run; somewhere sometime a squirrel drops dead.

Cats. Dogs. Birds. Birds die in numbers. Your chainsaw? Snowmobile? Lawnmower? Truck? People kick the bucket all over the place. It's like, "Look out for Harry. Ya' almost stepped on Harry." Are you or are you not really sure; the blood clot; the aneurysm building up mass in you isn't brought to you C.O.D. carbon dioxide-rich blood? Well? Let me suggest, leaves and grass bear oxygen. If not, (and yet we destroy forests) (mow fields of grass over and over and over) if not the pipes. The pipes in the chest. Pipes, pumps, valves, and Alpha Dog 1; the big-hearted muscle in the center of your chest begins to clamor for air. Yeah, don't they raise hell?

And you say, don't quibble. I say monoxide—you say dioxide. Name your poison. When 'they' were passing out brains I thought 'they' said trains, and I said, "I'll take a long, slow one . . ." Well the truth is, I live a long slow life. So if I had an embolism in my brain, I could maybe survive a mild stroke, or petite mal-seizure.

I'll tell you one thing. I never killed an oxygen-rich,

life-giving tree knowingly. God help people who do or did. I hardly even ever mowed the lawn with a power mower. Hardly ever.

Yeah, I walk where I go. Circulate the blood. Filter waste. Consumption by-products. Nobody is going to tell you this on a 1-800-Love Connection. Breathe deep. Relax.

Buttons

I have good news, and I have bad news. What's that? You want the bad news first? Okey, dokey. There are world leaders with their finger on the 'button.'

Part of the good news now? Yes, part of the good news now, and only part of the good news because it's going to have to stretch a good long way to make up for that bit of bad news.

Part of the good news about 'buttons' is maybe you hit the 'button' right on the nose. This isn't sooo bad as long as you aren't thinking 'nose' literally, as in %Button, %Button, %Button, %Who's got your %Button . . . % Showing a kid the tip of your thumb through your fist; making the kid have hysterics; which, again, at this point and time we hope hitting the 'Button' isn't a kid's nose. We reverently hope not. Anyway, you pushed my 'Button.' I didn't mean to pole-axe you in half, in your car, ruptured screaming metal, as loud as you. If it's any conciliation, you pushed my 'Button.'

Never you mind I was 'buttoning' the top 'buttons' on my dress shirt on the way to work. The teenie weenie 'buttons' used to hold down the tie. Never mind too, I was going 66 M.P.H. in a 65 M.P.H. zone. I win—you lose. Teach you a little something about pushing someone's 'Button.' Take a chainsaw to you if you bellyache about it too.

'Button' your lip. This classic lost the sarcasm it was meant to convey along the way; please be silent. Don't ask.

Don't tell. The new 'Hush-Up.' It's mind boggling. Anyway, again, 'Button' out. I mean that in a different way, but I can't type it or say it. 'They' worked on me with blowtorches, and hammers, and bats. And now the arthritis will hardly let me do nothing.

'Butt' out? Don't interrupt? I can't remember. When I try to remember, I begin to shudder. The shuddering makes the arthritis worsen. Bottom out? Help.

The Hooker

That's what he was called; The Hooker. Even at the tender age of fourteen I knew if you wanted to piss off a serial killer—call him a Hooker. His hook is as narrow as an ice pick and just as strong. And speaking of strong, before I caught the Hooker, it was discovered he carried the drugged women, from the initial chasing down to the hooking, over one shoulder, sometimes as much as seven miles from downtown Chicago to the storm drains where he kept his 'catch.'

The monstrous things he then proceeded to do to his 'catch' the papers carried. From all accounts—the stench was hideous.

I knew about medicine and serial killers; and hideous and hookers from True Enquirer and Tabloid Yellow papers I found under my dad's mattress.

The Hooker struck in the fog, (in keeping with creeps). With him I must have seemed as though no challenge. We live halfway between Chicago and where the site of the carnage was eventually discovered. Me and Dad knew anyway. Dad's a detective on the Chicago Police Force.

Call me Bait. I'm the lamb to the slaughter. The sacrificial lamb. I have freckles from one side of my rosy cheeks to the other; and my eight brothers don't call me a tom-boy for nothing. I was in the front lawn on April 7th, in a lot of fog that had drifted in from Lake Michigan. I was pretending to wash the dog. There were eight detectives watching every move I made. I was wired.

I made the collar—and I made the bust. When he came at me, I kicked him in the balls, at the same instant I chopped him across the nose and simultaneously drove the palm of my hand up INTO his nose. The detectives had to pull me off him.

The Nail

It had happened so long ago. I was looking for nails for a box car in a junkyard called Moose Hill with my younger brother when a nail poking up out of a board goes in my foot halfway through—if you can imagine. Shit. I was okay.

I was in grade school. It was summer vacation. Grade schoolers on summer vacation forgot things quickly—in case you've forgotten.

Well, anyway I hardly felt it by the time a 'short-week' was up. Five days. Me and my brother Bill called five days a 'short-week.' But I'll tell you, I walked around mighty gingerly during that time.

The first thing that I noticed (that wasn't quite up to snuff) was that although I wasn't sad, I couldn't keep from crying or tearing up. After about a week of wetting through my eyes, time started to play tricks on me. At first I made a little joke out of it. I said things like, "It's been three years of a day Bill." I admit—I was sarcastic, but time seemed to run on and on. Billy responded, "What the hell are you talking about, Joe?" Billy is outspoken. I had no answer. Time fell off the chart. An hour was an eternity.

Pain was next. Excruciating pain is mild to what continues to wreak havoc in my body. If I got numb from the horrible pain, the pain leaked through the numbness. Poured. But by then I could no longer scream. My jaws had clamped shut. Lock jaw. But Lock jaw as in LOCK, did not end there—oh no, no, no. Parts of my body locked up. And now continue to lock up. And yet, the pain continues to gush past the lock ups . . . and worsens . . . worsens . . . ahhhh . . . ohhhh . . . unhhhhh . . .

The Problem

"I want you guys to start calling a 'situation' a 'problem.' Got it?" I was talking to hard cops. Street men. Road crews. These people were mean and I had to be just as tough.

Some of the veterans had leveled scatter-guns at the stomachs of punks and then blew the punk away because he had twitched at the wrong time.

Some of the old brass had been busted down for holding a teaser just a little too long on a perp. Short-circuits the bastard quick. Occupational hazard.

Two rookies climbed the ranks once because they were strung out on amphetamines to be alert for their shift; they got a call to a park assault. They found a punk kicking a guy on the ground. Thinking there might be other punks around, they cuffed one hand of the punk and then together lifted him up and told him to cuff his other hand to an overhead branch. By the time the rookies got back, the kid had to have his hands cut off for gangrene poisoning. The squad shared quite a laugh over that one. Life in the fast lane.

"Call a situation a problem?" There was sarcasm and irony. "Sarge? I got a problem." The voice in the back of the room spat dry humor. "I just shit myself!"

"Knock it off, Ramarez," I barked. This isn't funny. They're going to beat Denamorra. Beat Denamorra. Police lingo for jail break. Riot. Hunger Strike. The Squad Room went still. Lock down. Twenty-four hour guard duty. Death. Denamorra. Synonymous with Criminally Insane.

Up is Down. In is Out. Black is White. If you club one of those Bastards—don't stop until he isn't moving—and then club him some more.

"I want a show of hands for extra duty!" Every hand in the squad bay went up.

The Claw

Clyde was pushing his beat-up Dodge pickup out of a ditch when I came up upon him. Huffing and puffing he said, "Give me a hand, Geoffrey." I'm Geoffrey Collins and Clyde Weisblott is a step down from man on the evolution scale. "Push and steer, Clyde." He might have grunted okay or unhuhhh. I couldn't be sure which. I pushed backwards against his closed tailgate, with my legs first bent at the knees, and then taking mincing baby-steps backwards. Once we got his truck back on the road, I asked him what the hell was going on. We had a mild June night. Not two feet of snow.

"I saw a claw, Geoff. A whole damn paw, but at first all I saw was the claw." He was sweating. He was scared. "It's in that tree back there; eight or nine feet up." I went to look. I almost puked. The claws were stuck at the tree with maybe a foot of raggedy bear paw. There was blood everywhere. "What did it, Geoffrey, huh? What did it?" I'm kinda an outdoors type but I've never seen anything like that.

We called a Zoologist. Something tore the leg off a Grizzly Bear. What the hell happened to the rest of that bear?

The Trick

Simple. That's what Benny said, "Simple." "It's a lead-pipe-cinch to trick an old widow out of her loot." He didn't count on the x-factor, Benny didn't. I fell for Mary. I got an itch for her the first time I saw her; and by the fourth or fifth time I saw her, (while we planned this 'shake-down' right in front of her innocent round brown eyes) I was hooked. She was *appealing.*

I saw her in my mind's eye stretching languishingly up against me, almost as though a cat while dancing. Matching me step for step, on a stroll through a park. Elderly? Slightly. I'm no spring-chicken myself.

So Benny said, "Are you in? Do I have to read you the riot act?"

"Yeah, yeah."

"Okay, so listen up. Her old man died. His name is Ralph. He has a brother in Des Moines, Iowa. Ralph left George and Mary seven million dollars to divide between themselves. There's no other family. Here's the good part, Bob, Mary never met George; never even saw him. Ralph and George couldn't even agree on the time of day. No pictures of brother George laying around. So you kill George, become him, and with me as the attorney for the estate, we walk away with three and a half million."

What I did instead was murder Benny. Marry Mary. And move in with my new brother-in-law in Des Moines, Iowa with my charming wife.

The Plant

Bristo Bristo's factory processed and bottled all the wine 'fit to drink' in the three county area of eastern New York specifically in the townships of Congress, Vanity, and Whilom. The three counties in eastern New York are the ones northeast of the St. Lawrence. The towns are unscrupulous and full of rumor mongering; back-stabbing and cutthroat behavior.

Rot-gut. Mad Dog 20/20. (Not a vision in sight). Ripple. (Not a twittering laugh). What festered within the pricey dark glass was a sort of algae. You could pour it in a glass and pretend it was the 'Strawberries and Champagne Hour'; or you could call a spade a spade. You're a wino.

Now there is always a port in a sailor. A storm in a port? Or a sailor in a storm. So you punch in at the factory, and you pour vats of bubbly into bottles only fit for Molotov cocktails, and punch out. And hit a bistro, bar, gin mill, slop-shoot. And since you worked real hard making the booze—you might just as well guzzle it down. Isn't it party 'til you puke? Did you ever drive blind drunk? Hear things that go bump in the night?

Check it out champ. Staff workers in detox centers might have to wrap you in wet blankets. Slip a cog? Blow a fuse? A straight jacket when staff feed you creamed corn is but a giggle away. What happens when the party's over? Embolism? Aspirate? Sometimes you have a case of the screaming meemies. D.T.'s Delirium Tremens. When perhaps you see mad rats out of the corners of your eyes? So, what's your pleasure???

The Writer II

I'm a writer. I authored Peabody, Finch, and Studies. There was a time not long ago when I didn't care what I wrote. What I said. What I did, said, or wrote. I'm a freelance journalist who covered four wars. Wrote to *Newsweek* that Sgt. William Rafferty up on the Mekong Delta in '65 got half his face blown off. The brass said, "Kid's lucky to be alive." I had to write this shit. Or Pvt. Johnson will never walk again because of tripping a booby-trap in Afghanistan.

I wrote Medows and Medows. Maybe you've heard of them? A law firm such as, Peabody, Finch, and Studies? I say I wrote them. I say I authored them. I wrote them long histories of guys pinned down in bunkers. Rice paddies. I wrote of aggressive assaults by 'Charlie' hurling Chinese R.P.G. rounds into our compounds in some god-forsaken jungle or another. Hurtling plastic-explosive-laden jeeps into mortar, mud, and plaster walled hovels. Maiming Bobby, Johnny, Jose.

Yeah, I write to law firms. I write to insurance companies. The press. I write books.

I said I'm a writer and an author but I won't disclose my identity. I'm ashamed of myself. I don't quite feel like I did my part. I have no arm or legs, but I can tell a secretary to write things down. I can't carry grenades but I can say, "Hallelujah!"

The Pill

There were two Sleepers. 45 in each bottle. 90 Pills to get a little rest. There were four Mood Elevators, but how her mood was supposed to get Elevated was anyone's guess. 200 Mood Elevators. Four bottles each containing 59 tablets.

On the nightstand Ethel could easily spot the two bottles of Psychotropic Medications for Psychotic Episodes. Dr. Lance assured her, "Relax. Ethel, You're in good hands with Captain Midol."

So what do I do if I get a headache from taking all of this Malarkey? Get my stomach pumped? She paused in these stray thoughts because something had caught her attention. There was a bright green and yellow type Gel-Cap sort of pill laying on the nightstand where there had been only pill bottles moments before.

Ethel took it. She dry swallowed it before she had a chance to change her mind. She swept it up and dry swallowed it. She gagged slightly, but it went down. She thought it was going to have an immediate affect—it didn't. Nothing happened. Nothing happened, but Ethel blinked, and there was suddenly another bright green and yellow pill sitting there. "No. It's not there." And she dry swallowed this one too. And she took the next eight pills that fell from the sky or that came up from out of the sewer.

And then Ethel did an amazingly smart thing. She called Dr. Bruce Lance and explained the situation. Taking pills without knowing what they were for or what kind they were even.

Ethel got better. It was a psychotic episode. Dr. Lance monitored the medicine, and Ethel recovered.

Class Action

Of a necessity I have to encapsulate an awful lot of material in a short period of time. I get "The Chair" tomorrow. I want to get the 'juice.' Four or five consecutive death sentences, if it was possible. I got God. Before I got God, I killed a pimp.

He put my kid sister out on the streets. I was in the Army blowing the shit out of gooks. Bastard did that to MY sister? So they put a sealed indictment on my ass. A gag order. Don't brag on the knifing of that pimp. Don't talk to my sister about the good tricks.

So now, they go through my mail. Screen my visitors. They don't give you a fat T-bone in the A.M., before lights out, either. Hold your breath sucker. Sit on your hands. So, yeah, I cut that bad man. I had a plan. I was figuring, since I'd been in the Army, they'd maybe stick me in a stockade or a warfront. But, oh no, no martyrs in our Army. Then I'm thinking, put me in a firing squad—facing it, mind you.

So I'm sitting there thinking, as mainly all you can do is sit and think and a guy knocks on the bar.

"You can go to Heaven," he says.

"You can go to Hell," I said.

"Come clean," he said.

"Beat it," I said.

But something happened. Tough was over. I suddenly didn't care. I was swept with relief. It was a Spirit. Cleanliness. I said, "If this is the end, I want it forever."

He said, "It's God."
I said, "Who are you?"
He said, "CHRIST."

The Fish

I'm an average guy. I like baseball. I like football. I like women. I like to go fishing. Me and Gary hit the lake four or five times a week. Gary's got part of a college education, and I'm a dummy.

My name is Mike Reynolds and one day I had a dream I was a perch. A perch is a fresh-water game fish. Gary calls them 'Pesky Perch' but affectionately, like. Anyway I'm an open book with Gary too. It seems I blab about everything, too. Everything. I told Gary about the dream of me thinking I was a fish and in his deep throated, laughing way, he said, "You're also a Big 'Dummy,' Mike."

At the time I told Gary the 'fish dream' I casually mentioned I have an inordinate fear of fishhooks. You may ask yourselves, "Do you have an inordinate fear of fishhooks, Mike Reynolds?" The answer is a resounding, why, no, of course not. I just like to hear myself rattle on and on like some kind of 'Big Dummy.'

Well, after I calmed myself of the ensuing paranoia of Gary 'hooking' me, for one dumb reason or another, I casually mentioned I boffed his ole lady.

It took awhile to surgically remove the fishhooks he had put in my coffee. And I'm thinking he calls his gal Pearl and there's a set of railroad tracks outside his backdoor. . . .

Nose Job

Yeah, oh yeah. I've heard it all before. When they were passing out noses—I thought they said roses, and I said, "I'll take a big red one." Or, "What's that lump on your face . . . ?" "Oh, that's your nose." How about this oldie but goodie? "If your nose went on strike, would you pick-it?" Bathroom heh heh.

Yeah, I'm a plastic surgeon and since I immersed myself in my work thirty years ago, women have come in my office, bawling their eyes out—gently dabbing their noses. Why? Because they want me to smooth a razor thin 'character-line.' Remove a blemish. Fill a scar. These women will save for years for an appointment to see me. Diet to save money on eating. Give up smoking to save money on tobacco. Give up drinking. Live in the cold to save on heating bills.

Hell hath no fury like a woman scorned.

They are told, these desperate women, by selfish, sarcastic husbands and boyfriends, "I smell blood . . ." Or another time honored colloquialism directed at the fairer species—"I smell money . . . !"

Well, sitting in the waiting room today is a fair man. He has light brown hair. Hazel eyes. Full parted lips in a slight smile. He is reading a *Newsweek*. There is no appointment scheduled for him or anyone else today; so, my curiosity was piqued.

I said, "May I help you?" My office manner is professional and courteous, and yet, when he answered, my stomach tightened cruelly and ached.

He said, "Why do you doctors have to be so nosey?"

Cool

I had the Feds fooled for a long time. I'd told the subjects that I had a teleporter. I had a killer. And that was totally brainwork. I'll admit, at first, what I did to some of my friends—and enemies, (enemies were easy) was done through the power of suggestion. Hypnosis. Hypnotics. That sort of thing.

Billy got me upset. He fell in the second category of people. Enemy. Kept saying, "Cool." "Cool dude." He was the first to go. I have to hand it to old Billy, he was resilient. Clung to life for a good six months maybe. He bugged me. Got under my skin, you might say. The hard-core docs subscribe to the idiom, you can brainwash someone to be susceptible to hypnosis, power of suggestion, hypnotics.

I studied medicine in my first ten years of college. Medicine. Pharmaceuticals. I majored in it. I could sedate with Penethol, remove a limb, dress the removal site, keep the subject, 'under', until the stump re-knit. Then I awaken Billy and I say the limb is stuck in limbo, but don't worry, we'll go back and fetch it. If it's a particularly fine limb, or organ, I pass it around for awhile. After all, share and share alike.

The recipient of a leg today may be the donor of a liver tomorrow. Cool Dude.

You have to watch yourself. Sometimes someone isn't satisfied with their slice of the action. They want a bigger donation. A trunk? A parcel? Yep. Cool Dude. Road Pizza? Nothing goes to waste. Waist. Pun intended. Yeah. Yeah. So keep it right people—keep it right. You might end up looking like a jigsaw puzzle. Or the lack of essence of you. Cool Dude.

The Time

I used to say in this big city, (pick a big city; all the big cities are pretty much like all the rest of the big cities) they wouldn't give you the time of day in one. Well whether this is the case or not, I took to checking my shadow on the sidewalks. Did you know you cast a shadow at night? Yeah, between street lights. Longer just beyond them. Shorter the closer you approach the next one.

But during the day. During the day. The time honored habit of glancing skyward to the sun—to check its whereabouts? To maybe check the position in the sky for a possible time reference? To maybe observe the shadows of buildings in your proximity as a time frame from their shadows?

Stay with me here. Distances between streetlights when shadow is least or longest may make a tedious type walk a bit more comfortable. Watching the shadow lengthen or shorten. Or mentally calculating the time it took to reach from one street light to the next. Or counting your footsteps may pass the time somewhat.

Another manner in which to pass time. A cloud passes over you. Under the sun. Count the seconds it takes to pass or until the next cloud takes to pass overhead. Little amusements, initially. After a time you're counting. Counting and counting. Counting everything. Before long you've expanded other awarenesses also. The direction from which the wind blows. How fast?

You may say, "What a waste of time," and you'll get no argument out of me. BUT, have you heard the glad word? All in God's TIME? There's a reason I'm telling this.

There is a well documented method of reaching shelter just before a storm. Other than the obvious, T.V., radio, newspaper.

The way is to count the seconds between clashes of thunder when the sky darkens just before a storm. Count, one, one thousand; two, one thousand; three, one thousand. For each 'one thousand' allow one minute of real time. 'So, let's say you get up to five one thousand—you have about five minutes 'til a cloud burst.

The Book

My name is Savage, Mike Savage. I can't believe what happened to me. I get the shudders even thinking back about it. I wrote a book.

I'm an average guy. I work an eight hour shift at the Sunoco gas station up the street. I drink a little beer and shoot a little pool after work. I go on a date once in a while. There's a casino in town and I thought, I'll write a book about it. What I did instead was start playing the slots and drinking there.

The working slowed down at the Sunoco station as the gambling increased. At first, incrementally and then frequently, and increasingly. Until things became a blur. I was drinking four days a week, and working two. One day Mike Schiffer, the foreman, called me to his office and laid it on the line. "Savage, I got to let you go!

"You're supposed to be here six days a week—but you're not—out!" There was no point in arguing. I left. Before I did, I said; "I'm writing a book. Then I'll be famous. Then I'll be back!" I don't know if he was being funny or what, but Mike Schiffer said, "Don't make book on it." An advance. I can get a friggin' advance on my book.

Except the book was a disaster. Some goons came around from the low-grade publisher to 'negotiate' the return of the 'loan.' The bank sent lawyers for monies borrowed. I work for Mr. Schiffer. He's no longer. 'Mike,' I'm lower than whale shit. I work the shit jobs at lower than minimum wage and I'm made to feel I'm 'lucky' to earn that. You bet.

The Bricks

There was a proliferation of thoughts going through my head. Get a beer or two? Or save the money for a pack of smokes??? I had been walking the streets of Miami for three days and two nights. I wouldn't sleep on the streets—someone could cut your throat or shoot you. If a cop in a cruiser happened to see you moving right along, he maybe thought you were going to work or heading home. If you ducked into a Citgo Station to 'comb your hair,' well, he than probably figured you had left the vicinity.

Anyway, I hadn't eaten in a day or two and I didn't mind. It's just that you're told not to drink on an empty stomach. There's no law against it yet. Besides, maybe I could relax enough to curl up in some alley. I could borrow butts in the bar.

The bar was loud. Loud and garish. Strobe lights. Knee-deep fog. A strung out rock band from hell was making a cacophony in one corner. A mix of Heavy Metal and Acid Rock. They reached a crescendo. There was a lot of tiffany percussion.

A girl of about fifteen with a leather mini-skirt, eye-brow rings, lip rings and no top; no top on top, said, "Beer?"

"Bud," I answered reflexively. This girl was in serious trouble. The girl bought me the beer. "What's your name, mister?" I was going to get myself in a mess here.

"I'm Bill." "I'm Julie." She offered her hand but I just

91

looked down. "Don't worry, you can crash in back with the band." She then did an amazing thing; she gave me twenty dollars. It was like hitting the lottery. My arm tingled. I said, "You're an angel."

A smile tugged at the corners of her mouth and she said, "Have fun, Bill."

Sports

Class AAA ball wasn't anything new to me. I had played triple A ball in the corps. Baseball. Football. Marine Corps. Thirty years ago. They play blood and guts ball in the Corps. It's fun.

I played triple 'A' in the service between my military duties. Guard duty. Close order drill. Maneuvers. Mess duty.

I was thinking at the time: I can supplement my military pay by writing.

Besides; I like military life.

Did I say I'm in the brig? It seems I maybe pushed myself a bit too hard.

Broke down. Did I say I hear voices? Too too bad. Yeah. Too too bad when one of those young soldiers is in tow and the 'voice' yells, "Drag 'im in the car." "Pummel to silence." "Pulverize in woods." Yeah, too bad. Those thirty guys will never tackle me again. Never block the basket.

I'm what? Going to get a firing squad? Soldiers are supposed to get shot.

Oh, bad Sgt. Bob, shot a civilian. Decorate him. It's hell out there. Give him a medal. Give him a promotion.

Maybe I used my bat the wrong way a little too much. I'm sorry, okay? Now let me go. I said I was sorry and now I just want to have a little fun. Hear a ref or ump yell "Play ball." Maybe drown out some of the orders in my head.

Tubed

There was nothing I could do. I was being sucked into my television. I wasn't always being sucked into my television, and at this point I would say, "Thank God"; but, I no longer much believe in God. Besides, maybe I'm not so much being sucked into my T.V. as being used around in my house by Mr. Lovely. My computer. Electricity run haywire by radioactivity. Is this your hypothesis, Mr. John Jenkins? Yes sir. Indubitably. Mr. Lovely Computer. On a scale of 1–10, Mr. Jenkins, how do you rate Mr. Lovely? Indispensable. It'll make you a pot of coffee and drink it for you. Till it forces you about. The eyeballs draining should have been the first clue. Blurred vision. Dizziness. Stumbling. Swimmy sight. Drippy nose and eyes.

Something ain't quite right. And in the wee hours of night? Do we see what we think we see? Diodes blinking. Winking far away in the distance. In a disturbed sleep? Do we squint to see these bright reds, yellows, and greens?

Oh yes I should think we squint to see these brightly colored lights. Do we sweat so much it leaks in our sleeping nightmare filled eyes? Do we sweat so much to see the pretty lights that it *pours* in our eyes? Yes Mr. John Jenkins; I should think it does.

And John Jenkins, doesn't Mr. Lovely, the on again-off again computer, tell us to download ream after ream of facts and figures? And doesn't Mr. Lovely now order us to increase by dozens upon dozens of percentages of documents and files? Within Mr. Lovely; ITSELF?

And as per *suggested* in the wee hours as well, have we or have we not been moving our chair closer and closer to the television screen? And finally, Mr. Jenkins, doesn't what started out feeling like harmless static electricity now feel as though bolts of voltage?!?

Full

Hydrophobia: N. 1. Rabies; Webster's American Dictionary. College Edition. c. 2000.

Yeah; I'd gotten bitten by those rats in the sewer and they gave me rabies.

But, they *did* something to me. There's no question about the fact that I'd gone mad. Being trapped and half eaten alive by rats would drive you mad too. But, that's not what I mean that they had *DONE* something to me.

I itch terribly. There are times I feel like scratching myself down with a wire brush. I can bear no moonlight. I can tolerate no liquids, although I thirst as a madman. I return to the ruins when the moon rises. I return to the ruins, climb through the gratings to the sewer canals and hiss at my distorted reflection in the filthy sewage until morning.

My name is Maxine. Maxine Common. I was on a photo-journalist assignment to find out if bats and rats would co-exist in the sewers under Manhattan.

And why or why not. I found Raoule three days ago, back in a tunnel.

Rats, cockroaches, maggots and flies were making a veritable feast out of what was left of poor Raoule. What killed him? You would ask a half madwoman what happened to poor Raoule?

I'm keeping this conversation going on the Camcorder we have with us, but it's low on juice. I can't bear sunlight; I howl like a wolf. I've got other problems now, too. I sick up.

And down. All the time. And I cramp. Dehydration. Like a pretzel. The rats are bolder. They stare malevolently at me. "Oh God, I'm pregnant. . . ."

Oops

I'm a randy-assed trucker and I don't care one way or the other if you like it or not. Actually I'd like you not to like the fact that I'm a big bad randy-assed trucker so I could wrap my muscular arms around your scrawny-assed neck and flex.

I'm such a randy-assed trucker that nothing would give me greater pleasure than hearing your esophagus snap. Nobody asked you to care if I live or died; did they, sweetie? I'd just as soon shove Molly, my eighteen wheeler of burning rubber up your Chevy's ass—as breathe in and out.

Oh, Mr. Big Bad Truckerman is mad. Yeah, I'm mad. I was mad the first time they killed me too. It was those Seminoles. Yeah, maybe I was pressing the pedal to the metal in their town when I hit Grandma Moses. She isn't Grandma Moses, she's Irish/Dutch not Seminole—and for that I say, Thankee-Jesus.

The Seminole Indians laid a curse on me though. You've heard of Montezeuma's Revenge? Well I call this curse, Geronimo's Revenge. Three consecutive lifetimes of trucking mad. Three lifetimes of getting eaten by an alligator after three consecutive lifetimes of trucking mad. Three consecutive lifetimes of hitting Grandma Moses with Molly; after three consecutive lifetimes of trucking mad; three consecutive lifetimes of getting eaten by an alligator . . . after . . . after . . . after all the other futile pursuits of happiness.

Ya know what I can't get out of my head? What if Grandma Moses had been Seminole???

Luck

Sure, I'm lucky. I was given to understand that there are just so many averages. And basically just so many odds. Just so many odds and so many averages working for or against you. In Middle School I learned the law of averages and the odds of something usually work for you.

Sure. You can get hit by lightning. The odds are against it. But wouldn't you rather hit the lottery? I had a friend who said, There'll be a scalper at the gates of Heaven. He may just have a point there—he went to visit the ballpark upstairs???

But, dumb luck; if you'll stay with me here a minute, isn't the kind of luck I mean. My Aunt said she saw a frog get caught by a snake, the snake got caught by a bird before the snake could swallow the frog, and the frog leaping from the mouth(s) of the snake and bird before it was eaten, into a road, and squished by a car. Pretty shitty dumb luck.

But when I catch hell, I hope it's like that frog—quick. Scare the living daylights heeby-jeebys just before POP, but fast-fast.

I got slammed by a bullet. Sometimes I feel like I ended up in No-Man's Land-Purgatory. I took a .38 slug in my Umbligata. Brain damage big time. Paralyzed. I can't make anyone understand. I got bit (stung) in the eye a minute ago. It may have been a moment ago or maybe it happened 16 or 17 years ago. I'm paralyzed but I can shriek in my brain—what's left of it. A wasp. An African killer bee. The odds are against it? Unnnngggghhhh.

What's the average of something like this happening? Ohhhhh Ohhhhhh. Please be an African Killer Bee. . . .

Buddies

Yeah, I got my buddies. Books. Go ahead and laugh. I got mysteries. Westerns. Fiction. I got dramas. Poetry. And Classics. Yeah, I got classics. Don't leave out the classics. I got my book-buddies. I got journals i.e. see this which you hold. Sports books and comedy.

Why do I call my books my buddies? Why do I collect books? Why do I amass literature? Why do you collect toe-nail clippings? I don't know. How should I know? Oh, you think maybe I got a little cookoo over books. Well let me tell you a little something about cookoo. I once read somewhere in a dictionary that one definition of insanity is doing something over and over again, expecting different results. Well let me tell you a little something mister, when I read words over and over; I DO get different results; so, that must mean I'm not insane.

Thing is, started to eat everything I read. Newspapers. Books. Letters. Yeah, I'm blowing up. I'm big. Big as a house. But I'm not doing anything expecting different results about anything I'm doing! I eat books, and I expect to get big, and, I get big. But how do we get off the subject of insanity? That's something I can't seem to get any different results about. I hope I'm not getting lazy. Too lazy to look up another definition of insanity? For example?—Perish the thought. That would be border/line? Compulsion? Would somebody help me? I can't seem to find my dictionary.

360

180 Stories in two years. Yes short stories to be sure, but 180 stories, nonetheless. But that guy could write. The goal? To do 90 stories a year for four years. 360 short stories. Shipley's Believe It or Not. I can maybe do one a month—if someone lights a road flare under my ass.

90 Stories. I asked Bill Shortstacks why he did it. "They's in there." He lifted his filthy Pittsburgh Raiders hat and blew gin breath, while showing his large yellow, gapped teeth, chuckling. That explained it. "They's in there . . ." I went home scratching my head over that one; but I didn't stay home.

Bill Shortstack's shack lay between Cunningham Road and East Boulevard. Some Boulevard; junk cars in the driveways, some with only one tire; sometimes two. Sometimes the hood was up. Most of the tires were flat anyway.

The window was a cracked dirty mess. It would do. He ate a bug. He dangled a bug that looked somewhat like a cross between a beetle and a cockroach, over his thrown-back head, mouth open, said something to the bug and dropped it. Mr. Bill Shortstacks, writer of short stories, eats bugs! He turned his head and stared at me. I ran down his driveway to my car and threw up.

So Mr. Shortstacks plans to write four books of short stories, buy bugs from the Royalty checks and live, happily ever after. What were you thinking? At the point I caught him eating bugs, he was at #360. "They's in there. . . ."

The Stain

The stain was on the ceiling. Duh, that's where most of them are. "You butt-rust, you put a sock in your drain." The stink of the sock was going to be there a long, long time. It didn't stink real, real bad, anyway. What got me was the stain. I washed it. I scrubbed it. I painted it, but it was still wet. The perpetually wet stain. And although the stain didn't stink, it smelled like a dirty sock! So I scrubbed. I scrubbed and scrubbed and scrubbed. So I painted. I painted over the paint and scrubbed.

And the guy upstairs? Bangs on his floor. My ceiling. Knocks down dust onto my upraised, askance face. And the paint? All that paint? It gets in my nose and eyes, lungs, mouth and hair, as I look up to paint that stain. And I got to stop right here, girls and boys, and ask, "Are we having *fun* here, or what?"

Bang. Bang. Bang. So moron knocks loose his socks, goes around like Bab-A-Louie. I'll fix 'im. A pan of vinegar bought to a slow boil, would what? Rise? Twenty or thirty candles all burning at once would make swell stink rising. Twenty or thirty candles all blown out at once. A little banging on a pan with a large metal spoon? A lot of banging? Wake the dead, I tell ya. Crank the heat? Give Bozo a hot foot?

I could turn the T.V. up. I could turn on my shower and flush my toilet when he's in his shower.

Hey, hey, E-A-S-Y, you don't want to cause mayhem for a neighbor, do you? You bet your ass I do! Oh no, he's a cop. . . .

103